Delores Lowe Friedman

IAN'S PET

illustrated by Susan Magurn

HOUGHTON MIFFLIN COMPANY   BOSTON

Atlanta   Dallas   Geneva, Illinois   Palo Alto   Princeton   Toronto

One day at school,
everyone wanted
to write . . .

and draw . . .

and talk . . .
about pets.

2

Everyone but Ian.

Ian didn't have a pet.

Ian had
to write . . .
and draw . . .
and talk . . .
about a pet
that he wanted to have.

It was fun, but Ian wanted a real pet.

"Why don't you get a dog?" said Lou.

"Or a cat?" said Kim.

"I can't," said Ian.

"Not at my house."

One day, Ian was looking
at some frogs and thinking.

"Frogs aren't big — but a pet frog
wouldn't be happy.
But, look! I see fish, too!
A fish is just the pet for my house."

You can guess what Ian did.

Now Ian could write and draw
and talk about a real pet!

"This is my pet,"
he said,
"Fred the fish!"

8

Ian would write and draw
and talk about
Fred all the time.

Fred is getting bi

Fred wasn't like other pets.
Fred wasn't like other fish.
Fred was something special!

One day Lou said,
"I don't think Fred is a fish.
Fish don't look like that!"

"What can he be?" said Kim.

"I think Fred is a dinosaur!" said Lou.
"Ian said he wanted a dinosaur."

Fred is bigger.

But Fred wasn't a dinosaur,
and he wasn't a fish!

Fred is getting big.

My pet Fred the fish.

Fred is bigger.

14

Look at Fred.

Fred is not a fish.

Fred was a . . .

Surprise!

Fred was a frog.
And to Ian he was
something special!